CW00385867

Work Husband

-Written By-
Octavia Grant

Copyright © 2019 by Octavia Grant
Published by M-DOC Creations Publications, LLC

Cover Designer: Chy Seoul
https://www.facebook.com/groups/1432690323484292

TABLE OF CONTENTS

CHAPTER 1

"Oh My God!!!" I moaned as Lamar dug for gold in between my legs. If the feeling I was experiencing at the moment was sold in stores, I'd buy it every day. I was in a state of total bliss. If I had to rate how I was feeling on a scale of 1 to 10, the feeling would be 15. The sensations that were running through my body were so intense that I wanted to cry.

"Damn Crystal. You're wet as fuck." Lamar said as he pummeled inside of me with long deep strokes in the backseat of his Lincoln Continental. No man had ever set my body on fire the way Lamar did. As he bent down to kiss me, all I could taste was the sweet saltiness of my juices that lingered on his thick lips from feasting on me.

I needed more of him. Lifting my legs over his shoulder. I raised my butt off the leather seats so I could get all 9½ inches of him inside of me. I knew what Lamar liked, so I slowly grinded in circles while contracting my muscles.

"Damn Crystal." He moaned as he began to pound harder with no mercy. The car rocked and shook like a mini hurricane was forming on the inside. Even though his car had 5% limousine tints on the windows, and no one could see in, it was obvious what was happening on the inside.

Personally, I didn't care who saw us. Wherever Lamar pulled it out at, was where it was going down at. It didn't matter to me that I was a married woman. It didn't matter that we could get caught. The only thing that mattered to me was Lamar Santana. I needed him more than I needed air to breathe.

"Baby, I'm about to cum." I screamed as my body stiffened, then shook like I was having a seizure.

No matter how many times we had sex, anytime I started to cum it felt like the first time all over again. Grabbing me by the waist and pumping harder and faster. Lamar threw his head back and growled like a wounded bear as he filled me to capacity with his cum.

My face and body were drenched from the sweat that dripped from his thick body. His chest rose and fell as he took deep breaths trying to calm his racing heart.

"Are you trying to kill me?" He asked while looking at me like he wanted to go another round. His dick was still hard like he hadn't just emptied his ball sacks inside of me. Streams of cum dripped from his dick onto his beige leather seats. As I stared at his long thick manhood glazed with our cum, I started to salivate.

I could not get enough of this man, and I was not about to let that hard dick go to waste. Without saying a word, I got on my knees in the back seat of his car and took his whole 9½ inches into my mouth.

"Mmmm." I moaned as I wrapped my tongue around the head of his dick. His body stiffened and he hissed as I sucked him slowly. He tasted so good that I wanted to savor it. His dick got harder as I sucked him like a vacuum. All I could hear was my slurping, but I knew he was moaning by the way he gripped my hair. My goal in life was only to satisfy this man.

Everything about him turned me on. His chocolate skin was flawless. Low Caesar haircut, full beard, and eyes so light brown that anytime he looked at me I felt like I'd lose my breath. Husband or not, this man was mine.

"Come sit on this dick. Let me get another one before its time to go," he said as he pulled my head off his dick. I wasn't ready to stop sucking on him, but I would do whatever he asked me to do. Straddling his lap, I slid him into my back door.

"Ahhh!!!" we said in unison as his thickness entered my tightness. Anal sex had been something we indulged in from time to time. But often enough that the pain was nonexistent.

"This dick is so good baby." I said as I bounced hard on his lap. Most women couldn't handle backdoor action, but I took the whole thing like a pro. Lamar trained me well. I knew what he liked, needed, and wanted to be satisfied and I had no problems fulfilling his needs. It felt so good that I could feel cum dripping from between my legs and sliding down his shaft.

Lamar's face twisted and locked into a grotesque mask as his second nut, got ready to expel from the tip of his dick. Grabbing me by my waist for the second time. He pumped harder inside of me until he emptied his load into my anal canal.

"God damn!" He screamed. "What the fuck are you trying to do to a nigga?" He asked out of breath for the second time. His perfect white teeth gleamed, and his deep dimples showed above his beard line. This man was perfection.

"You already know what I'm trying to do. I'm trying to keep all those other bitches out your face." I said as I leaned down and attempted to kiss his thick lips.

Instead of allowing me to do so, he turned his face slightly. I frowned at the blatant disrespect. I knew why he did it, but that didn't mean I had to like it.

"Really, Lamar? Are you serious?" I asked as I got off his now limp dick. I was furious, but I tried hard to conceal it.

"Come on Crystal, you know good and well that I'm not going to kiss you after my cum was in your mouth." He said as he pulled his clothes on.

I already knew that, but that didn't mean I had to like it. I kissed him after he went down on me with no problem. But, instead of arguing with him, I sucked my teeth and pulled my dress over my head with major attitude. I wasn't about to argue, but he could definitely get the silent treatment.

"Stop acting like that Crystal. How long have we been doing this? You know my likes and dislikes. Nothing has changed since day one. So, fix your face and adjust your attitude so we can go back in here and act like we weren't just having sex." Lamar said and walked out of his car and back into our office.

CHAPTER 2

"Damn Mrs. Jones. I thought you were taking a 2-hour lunch break." Trinity said as she stood next to my cubicle smiling hard like she had a secret or suspected that I had one. Lately she had begun calling me 'Mrs. Jones.' I'm not sure why. But I wished she'd stop. It's like she was trying to find new ways to get under my skin.

"I'm sorry Trinity. My car stalled again, and I had to wait for roadside assistance to come and jump my battery." I lied. There was absolutely nothing wrong with my car. David bought my car off the showroom floor, but that was the only lie I could think of that sounded plausible.

"Is that right?" She asked, looking at me like she knew I was lying. I know what she wanted me to say. But I refused to say it. My personal business was mine. I refused to share my personal life with anyone in my office. Unless it was Lamar.

"Yes, Trinity. My battery needed to be jumped." I said as I looked at the emails on my computer screen. Trinity was starting to get on my last nerve. If she didn't get out of my face, I was going to throw the anger I had for Lamar at her.

"It's so weird that you always have battery issues, when your husband just bought you a brand-new car." She smirked. I snapped my head in Trinity's direction and looked at her as if she had just lost her mind.

"And just how are you so well versed on what and when my husband bought something for me? Are you the third wheel in my marriage?" I asked as I stared at her with the look of death.

I wouldn't be surprised if David was or had been fucking my co-worker. That was just the type of lowdown shit his ass would do. But whether he did or didn't I no longer cared.

Trinity looked as if she was stunned and taken aback by my tone. I could see the apprehension running through her head as I glared at her.

"I didn't mean any disrespect Crystal. I just remember you saying that even though your old car was giving you so much trouble, you weren't going to buy a new one because it was already paid for.

So, when you came to work in a brand new one, I just assumed that your significant other bought it for you. All I was trying to say is if your car is giving you so much trouble, maybe you should take it back to the dealership and have a mechanic check under the hood for you," Trinity suggested with a shrug.

Her little colloquialisms were getting on my damn nerves. But instead of slapping her and telling her to mind her own business, I simply turned back to my computer screen and shook my head at her transparent ass.

"Maybe I'll take your advice and do that." I said without looking at her.

I could feel her staring at me, but I refused to acknowledge her presence. Trinity was the equivalent of an annoying house fly. She kept flying around and no matter how many times I swatted her away. She always came back.

"Lamar also came back from lunch late. Not as late as you were. But still late none the less. It seems like anytime you're late he's late too. I guess it's just a coincidence. I guess your team can do whatever it wants to do." Trinity said.

Instead of paying her any attention I focused on the work in front of me. Trinity, like so many other people in the office were extremely curious about me and Lamar. We were so close, but our lips were sealed. I'd never discuss my personal life with any of the females in this office. They didn't need to know what was going on between the two of us.

I was a firm believer in keeping your private life private. Ladies nowadays were scandalous and the moment you told them about how a man was knocking the lining out of your pussy, they thought that was an invitation to try him out. No thanks. I wasn't ashamed to say that I'd kill a bitch behind Lamar Santana.

Just the thought of Lamar touching another woman had me so angry that I wanted to throw something. I made sure I gave him everything he wanted and needed. Another woman could never do for him what I did for him. So, there was no need for him to seek elsewhere.

RING!! RING!!

Hearing my ringing phone pulled me out of my trance. Just the thought of Lamar between the legs of another bitch did something to me that I couldn't explain. Looking at the caller id of my work phone, I sighed and sucked my teeth at seeing my husband's name and cell phone number.

"Modern's Advertising Firm. You've reached Executive VP Crystal Jones." I said into the phone. My husband David was the last person that I wanted to speak with. Especially after an action-packed hour-long lunch break with my work husband.

"What's up Beautiful. How is your day?" David asked. His deep voice commanded respect. There was a time when the sound of his deep voice used to get me soaking wet. But things had certainly changed for us. When our family of two became a family of three, by way of him having a child with a stripper, any love I had for David Jones went out the window.

"So far so good," I said without a trace of enthusiasm. He knew that things weren't the same between us. I had no idea why he even tried. The lavish trips he planned, the brand-new Lexus, and the new 5-carat wedding ring that he bought were all pointless gifts. He would've been better off paying for the divorce that I asked him for.

"Have you already had lunch? I'm on your side of town and thought we could get something to eat at the café by the Koi Pond." He said.

I could hear the pleading in his voice, but I didn't give a damn. He did this to himself, he did this to us, and I was not about to pretend like I was interested in discussing anything that he wanted to talk about. Fuck him.

"I've already gone to lunch and I'm busy. So, I'll…"

"Crystal. I'm tired of you cutting me off like what I need to say to you isn't important." David said cutting me off before I could even finish my sentence. "I fucked up. Are you going to hold that against me forever?"

"I told you what I wanted, and you shredded the papers. Like I said I'm busy David. I don't have time for this conversation. Especially when you already know what I want and why I want it." I said snapping back at him.

"Look, we'll talk about this tonight when I get home. And we will talk about it Crystal. 'Til death do us part. Right? I'll see you at home." David said and hung up.

"What the fuck? Was that a threat?" I asked myself. The nerve of this nigga. I never understood how men could fuck up a good thing. Then get mad, when the woman no longer wanted their ass. At one point and time, I loved David's dirty drawers. There wasn't anything that I wouldn't do for him. But now, I genuinely hated David's light skinned ass.

He wasn't used to a woman not wanting him. He was so accustomed to women being a fool for him that he didn't know how to accept a woman, yet alone his wife, telling him to fuck off. His catlike eyes, neatly groomed goatee, and wavy hair wouldn't save him this time. He could go to hell.

"Are you ok?"

I damn near jumped out of my skin when I heard Lamar's voice. I had no idea that he was even sitting at his desk. When I answered the phone, he was not there. Usually, I could tell when he was close by the scent of his Ralph Lauren cologne. But this time I didn't. David's stupid ass had me so worked up that I didn't even notice his presence.

"Yeah, I'm straight," I said throwing him a fake smile. Since I wasn't sure how much he heard, I didn't want to meet his gaze. So, I focused on my emails and the files that were on my desk. For the past few years, I had shared so much of my personal life with Lamar. So, I knew the tone of my voice had given me away.

He knew my mannerisms, moods, and behaviors. I don't know exactly what caused us to become so close, but I can't say I was unhappy about it. It was easy to talk to him. Even though I didn't always agree with his whorish and mannish way of thinking. I appreciated all the jewels that he dropped in my lap.

"I heard your whole conversation. So, you may as well tell me what's up. Because I might not want to hear it later." He laughed. It felt strange talking to him about things that went on between my husband and I. Especially after he and I had mind blowing sex in his car.

"Mr. Santana, thank you for checking on me. But I really am alright." I lied. Truthfully, I was in hell. I missed what David and I used to have. I thought we had a perfect marriage. But I was wrong.

"Ok." He said nonchalantly then looked at his phone and began texting. I knew he wasn't going to pressure me to tell him anything that I wasn't ready to talk about. But the thought of him possibly texting another bitch, made me unclasp my lips.

There was just something about Lamar. All the women in the office wanted a piece of him or attention from him. From the 18-year-old young ladies to the 60-year-old mature women. If they had a vagina, they wanted a piece of the 6'5" 300lb stallion. Too bad for them, because he was already mine.

The other females in the office wanted to know if Lamar was attracted to them, I already knew he was attracted to me. I caught the attention of most men, and even some women, with my caramel skin tone, long auburn hair, and hourglass physique.

"We're going to be signing the papers. I wanted him to sign them since I found out about the pregnancy. Now that he's decided to proceed. I don't know how I feel about it." I lied.

Since he said he heard my whole conversation, I had to make something up. Hopefully it sounded believable.

I refused to call my husband's name when I was talking to my other man. He deserved more respect than that. True, he knew I was married, but there was no need to throw that well-known fact in his face.

"Are you going to keep the same last name once your divorce is final? Or are you…"

I could see Lamar's lips moving but I couldn't focus on the words.

"How can you be so infatuated with someone you're already having sex with?" I asked myself. I had the biggest crush on a man that was already mine. I was so caught up in his eyes and his overall presence that his words didn't register in my ears. He sounded like the inaudible teacher on Charlie Brown. *Whomp. Whomp. Whomp. Whomp. Whomp. Whomp.*

Lamar's presence in my life was dangerous because I couldn't focus on anything when he was around me.

CHAPTER 3

"Why is this nigga so fine Lord?" I thought to myself as I watched Lamar's thick lips move. I knew he was talking but I was too captivated by his looks to even think straight. Anytime I was around him, I felt things that I shouldn't feel. But I couldn't help it.

For the past three years, Monday through Friday between the hours of 11am to 7pm, I was in agony. Never in my life had I ever gotten involved with a coworker. I heard several stories about office romances and rendezvous gone wrong. I knew better than to mix business with pleasure. But it was so easy to get caught up in the workplace.

For eight hours a day you had access to your coworkers' point of views. Which made you think you really knew the person on the other side of the cubicle. But usually, their 8-hour corporate persona was completely different from the person they were during the remaining 16-hours of the day.

Even though I knew that, when the opportunity presented itself for Lamar and I to take that plunge, I took it. 365 days later, here we were. Sitting across from each other, pretending like he hadn't penetrated every hole in my body.

As I watched his lips move, a scene from the 1990's sitcom Martin popped into my head. Martin told his fiancée Gina that he loved her 'soup coolers' meaning her thick lips. That was how I felt about Lamar's lips. Correction, that's how I felt about the whole package known as Lamar Santana. He was irresistible. I wish I didn't want him as bad as I did. I just couldn't help myself. He was my addiction. A habit that I was not trying to kick anytime soon.

"Crystal?!"

I damn near leaped out of my skin when I heard him calling my name. The deep bass in his voice pulled me out of my hypnotic state.

"H'uh? What?" I asked as I looked around the office puzzled. I knew I looked guilty of something. Like I was a child that had gotten caught with their hand in the cookie jar.

"Damn it Lamar. Why are you yelling my name like that? Especially when I'm sitting directly across from you?" I said with a major attitude. There was no reason for him to scare me like that. My heart was literally on the verge of jumping out of my chest.

"I'm yelling your name because I've been sitting here talking to you. Instead of you answering me, you're sitting there staring at me like a mental patient." He said and laughed. Heat radiated through my body at his words. I was so embarrassed. If I were a few shades lighter, I was positive that my cheeks and face would be beet red.

"You're slipping Crystal." I said to myself at the realization that I had been caught. Usually, I could sneak a peek at him then look away without him noticing. But today he was just a little more scrumptious than usual. I don't know if it was the powder blue Ralph Lauren button down and navy-blue slacks that turned me on.

Or was it his clean smelling cologne? Or the fact that he had just had his beard trimmed and maintained. Whatever it was, it had my juices flowing like The Nile.

My attraction to him was dangerous. So dangerous that it made me nervous. If I had to be honest with myself, I'd say I was dangerously in love with Lamar. But I didn't feel like being honest with myself at the moment.

"Boy whatever. Wasn't nobody staring at your conceited ass." I lied. I didn't care that he caught me. I wasn't going to admit it. I was pulling a page out of Jamaican Rapper Shaggy's playbook; It wasn't me. That was my story, and I was sticking to it. The scrunched up look on his face was so comical that I wanted to burst into laughter.

"Are you really going to lie to my face Crystal? Are you saying that I didn't just catch you watching me like a damn stalker?" he asked and folded his arms over his chest. Like he dared me to lie. Since he was daring me to lie, I did.

"That's right," I said as I batted my mink lashes. Instead of saying a word, he just shook his head. He knew I was staring at him, so a full dialogue about it was unnecessary.

"You are something else Crystal." He said and smiled showing off those pearly whites and dimples so deep, I could drink water out of them.

"I swear you guys' bicker like an old married couple. If I didn't know any better, I would've sworn David was in here with all the back and forth going on." Trinity said and laughed. This bitch was such a hater.

Maybe it was my imagination, but it seemed like she purposely tried to make me uncomfortable. I also hadn't missed that she always found a reason to bring my husband's name up. Like she knew him or some shit.

Ever since day one, she hated how Lamar and I meshed. He never spoke with anyone in this office the way he spoke to me. It was obvious that he had a real attraction to me and was only being nice to everyone else.

"Bony ass, hating ass bitch." I said to myself as I looked at Trinity like she was shit on the bottom of my shoe. Her saccharine laced smile was full of malice. It was obvious that she would do anything to get Lamar's attention. I couldn't stand this bony bitch. As if he could pick up on the negative energy in the room, he began to speak.

"That's Crystal. Sitting here acting like she ain't crazy." Lamar said and started throwing paper clips at me. He knew that I was about to get in Trinity's ass. Which is why he started throwing office supplies.

Joking around like this was one of the many reasons why I preferred being at work. It was a guarantee that I would get some laughs. Things had become so uncomfortable in my home. So, I enjoyed coming to work because it kept my mind off David.

"Yeah, it was her." Trinity said still being the third wheel in our conversation.

Without saying a word to Trinity, or even looking her way. I stuck my middle finger up at him and stuck my tongue out like a child.

"Mr. Santana. Let me make this clear for you. No one in this office wants your dark chocolate ass. I mean you're cute. But ain't nobody checking for you," I lied. The falsities rolled from my tongue like I was a natural born liar.

He looked at me and smirked, letting me know that he knew I was lying. The smirk on his face had my box overly sensitive. If I tried to walk, I'd have an orgasm. I hated that he had that effect on me. Something as simple as him saying: Hello, Good Morning or Goodbye had me dripping wet.

"Heyyyy Lamar." Penelope said as she walked through our office. Flirting with Lamar like he was King Shit. Trinity and I were less than a few centimeters away from him, but she neglected to speak to us.

"What's up Penelope? You're looking good today. How are you?" He asked smiling like a Cheshire Cat as the fake ass Nicki Minaj replica smiled in his face.

"This hoe." I said to myself as I frowned like I smelled something foul. She had her obviously fake silicone injected ass and breast all over my niggas desk.

"It's almost time to get out of here. What are your plans for tonight?" Penelope asked as she picked invisible lint off Lamar's shirt.

"A little of this. A little of that. You know how it is. I go where the action is." He smirked and leaned back in his chair.

"The nerve of this nigga. This nigga could be so fucking disrespectful at times. Flirting with this knock off bitch in my face. What kind of name was Penelope for a black girl anyway?" I asked myself as I glared at them.

Penelope was nothing more than a hood rat. Her 30-inch honey blonde Brazilian hair and light gray contacts did nothing to enhance her appearance. She was just an ugly duckling that thought she had a chance.

Several bitches were checking for Lamar. Even our Director of Sales went overboard to get his attention and it pissed me the hell off. I was so irritated that I found myself getting upset with Mr. and Mrs. Santana for creating a son as fine as theirs. Hearing Penelope giggle snapped me out of my trance. I was going to have to slap this hoe.

"You're so funny. You should…"

"Good afternoon, Penelope. How are you? It seems like you forgot to speak to Trinity and I." I said cutting her off and throwing mad salt in whatever game she was trying to spit. She was barking up the wrong tree and if she knew like I knew. She'd better find someone else's face to play in.

"Whatever," she scoffed. "I'll see you later Lamar." Penelope said as she sucked her teeth, rolled her eyes, and walked off.

"Fake ass bitch." I said to myself as I watched her extra-large butt cheeks move from left to right as she walked off. I was disgusted by her trashy demeanor. Bitches like her always felt the need to flaunt their fake assets just to get attention. Turning to Lamar, I glared at him with hatred in my eyes. He was becoming bolder with his flirtatiousness, and it was really starting to piss me off.

"Why do you always have to play in these bitches face?" I asked. I could hear the jealousy seeping out. I was about to lose my cool. His level of disrespect was starting to spike, and I didn't appreciate it.

"Jealous much?" he asked with a large grin on his face. I wanted to smack fire out of his sexy brown ass. Lamar could really be an asshole sometimes. During one of our many office talks, I remembered him saying that he was a rolling stone. If he knew like I knew, he'd better not

22

let me find out he was slanging dick to another bitch. Especially a bitch in this office.

"Alright guys. Now that you've gotten your end of the day ritual of arguing out the way. I have something to ask the two of you." Trinity said as she looked between me and Lamar. I didn't miss the mischievous look that crept over her face. Somehow, I already knew what the question would be.

"What is it?" Lamar and I asked in unison as we continued to stare at each other.

"You guys are always going back and forth, arguing like you're married. I mean I know you're married Crystal and Lamar I know you're seeing Andrea, but it seems like y'all have unresolved issues. Like a couple in heat. I'm just curious. But are you guys having sex?" Trinity asked, looking between the two of us. My body stiffened at the question that flew out of her mouth.

Though I was expecting it. I was still stunned by her brazenness. Trinity always dropped hints that she wanted to know if we were an item. But never had she come out and asked. Even though I was shocked, I was more stunned by the revelation of this Andrea character. Who the fuck was she?

"Crystal knows she's my work boo and I got love for her. But nah, I ain't never been in there. Y'all have a good night." Lamar said as he grabbed his car keys and walked   out   of   the   office.

CHAPTER 4

I was furious when I got in my car. For the past few years Lamar and I had discussed everything while we were at work. No topic was off limits. I knew that he preferred oral sex over vaginal sex before we even had sex.

I knew that his mother battled alcoholism after his father had an affair with her best friend and had a child. I knew that his father begged his mother to take him back after she was diagnosed with breast cancer. I knew so much about this man and his life. But I had no idea who the fuck this Andrea bitch was.

Pulling my cell phone out, I shot him a quick text. We never texted each other after work. I assumed it was because he knew I had a husband. I had no idea that the reason he wasn't communicating with me after work was because he had a woman at home.

Since David had begun checking my phone's activity, I couldn't save his number under his name. So, I scrolled down to the fake name that I had Lamar's number saved under and started to text him.

To: Monica From: Crystal Is there something you forgot to tell me?

To: Monica From: Crystal So you got a woman at home?

To: Monica From: Crystal Who the fuck is Andrea?

To: Monica From: Crystal How long has she been in the picture?

"The nerve of this nigga." I screamed as I logged into my social media accounts. I always logged out of my Snapchat, Instagram, and Facebook accounts. After I found out about the baby, David started going through my phone and checking my social media accounts, email, and pictures to see if I had been talking to anyone behind his back.

It was his guilty conscience playing tricks on him. After finding out that he was fucking bottom dwellers, I logged out of everything. David knew we were over. The sooner he accepted it, the better off him, his bastard child, and his stripper side bitch would be.

Opening the chat log on Snapchat, I typed another message to Lamar.

To: Santana_for_President From: CrystalJay *Nigga I know you see me blowing you up. Who the fuck is Andrea? Her pussy must not be the business since I get that dick all the time. Nigga keep fucking ignoring me. I'll have you on the front of a black Tee with angel wings.*

I copied the message and pasted it in his inbox on Facebook, his DMs on Instagram, and even found his Twitter and Myspace account from when he was 15 years old and pasted the messages there too. Anywhere I could think of reaching him I sent him a message.

"I refused to let another nigga play me." I said to myself squeezing the steering wheel so hard that my knuckles turned white. "And what did he mean by I'm his work boo?" I wondered to myself as I drove down the curvy road to my 3-story house. I was much more than a work boo, and Lamar was much more than a work husband. We were destined to be together. He had to know that.

Before we even had sex, he stayed on my mind constantly. I fantasized about him like I was a high school kid with a crush. I loved him. He was my first thought in the morning and my last thought before I went to bed at night. I had no idea who this Andrea bitch was, but I would make it my business and find out. If she thought she could have my man, she was sadly mistaken. By the time I made it home from work, I had sent Lamar over 30 text messages.

"One way or another, you will answer my questions." I said to myself as I pulled into my 2-car garage. Since David's car wasn't home, I didn't log out of my social media apps. Instead, I locked my car door and ran inside so that I could connect to the WiFi.

David bought me a car with WiFi connectivity, but the speed wasn't as fast as it was in the house. As soon as I entered my house through the garage door my mood went from bad to worse.

I sucked my teeth as I walked inside the home that was once my haven. A Little Tikes Cozy Coupe, doll baby, bassinette, and several little doll dresses were all over my living room floor.

A My Little Pony cup filled with purple juice and a half-eaten sandwich with chips sat on a My Little Pony plate on a toddlers table in front of the 65-inch 4K TV. Clear signs that David's daughter Nyla had been here. It was obvious that he rushed out with her, so she and I didn't cross paths.

"I'm not cleaning this shit up. It's his daughter." I said to myself and walked up the stairs to the bedroom that I had been occupying for the past twelve months. I knew I was wrong for hating a one-year-old, but I couldn't help it. David and I were married for five years, there should not have been a one-year-old running around. Especially one that I didn't give birth to.

When I used to bring the topic of kids up, he shut it down quickly. Saying he wanted to grow his business his first. He forced me to get two abortions saying the time wasn't right. Yet he planted a seed deep inside the womb of some stripper that was bleeding his ass dry in child support. That's what his thirsty ass got.

"Fuck him, that bitch, and their child." I said to myself as I wiped the tears that leaked from my eyes. I hadn't shed tears for David and our failed marriage in a while and I wasn't going to start tonight.

I needed to get my mind off David and the mess downstairs. I had more important things to worry about. Sitting on the edge of my bed. I pulled my phone out and went straight to the Facebook app. Since Lamar was ignoring my messages, I'd find out what I needed to know through his page.

Putting his name in the search box and opening his profile. I went to his friend list and typed in Andrea. Four beautiful profile pictures stared back at me.

"Let the games begin." I said as I went through all the profiles with a fine-tooth comb. I went through their pictures, their friends list, and even their wall post to see if Lamar had commented or liked anything. Nothing. I didn't see his name on anything that would make it look like he was dating any of these bitches.

"Who the fuck are these people?" I said out loud. I was so deep in Andrea's page that I forgot what I was originally searching for.

Hitting the back arrow several times, I came back to the original four pictures. I still had one more profile to go through. I stared at the last picture and hesitated. Andrea Turner's profile was the last of the four profiles that I needed to go through.

Looking at her picture, I felt my eyes begin to mist and I had no reason why. Nah, I knew why. Andrea Turner was everything that I wasn't. Very light, high yellow skin. Slim and petite. She wore her hair in a very edgy high low bob. She was beautiful. Just like Kamiya, David's baby mama.

"Why are you doing this Crystal? Do you really want to know the truth?" I asked myself. Without a second thought, I answered myself honestly, "Yes, I do."

Clicking on the profile, I searched through her pictures until I came across a picture that stopped my breathing. A picture of her with a couple of familiar young faces. Faces that hung on the pictures in Lamar's cubicle. His daughters.

Enlarging the picture, I hit the 'see more' link to read the description. It said, *'Mommy loves Lamaria and Larissa'.* My heart seized in my chest. This wasn't just some jump off, like Penelope. This was his baby mama. I assumed that they had a bad relationship since he never spoke about her. But I see now that I was wrong. I didn't know a damn thing about this bitch. Exiting her pictures, I went to her wall post.

"Son of a Bitch!!!" I screamed as I read some of the post on her page.

FB Post May 3, 2019 6:05am *Today marks 7 years. Have a great day at work Beautiful. Love you always. 81 likes 30 comments.*

FB Post May 3, 2019 9:13pm 7 *amazing years, 2 amazing daughters, 1 amazing man... I SAID YES!! 215 likes 107 comments.*

At the sight of the 3-carat engagement ring on her slender fingers in the picture next to the 'Will You Marry Me?" dessert.

I grabbed the lamp off my nightstand, yanked the cord out of the socket and major league pitched it against the wall. The clear lamp with turquoise blue, aqua blue, and beige seashells in the base shattered as soon as it hit the wall.

"This nigga tried to play me. He is mine," I screamed as I threw things against the wall in blind fury. After nearly ten minutes of insanity and looking at the mess I made. I began to cry. I loved Lamar with my whole heart, and he had a family that I knew nothing about. I mean yes, I knew he had kids. But I had no idea that he had a whole bitch too. Then an epiphany hit me. The tears in my eyes and the anger in my heart immediately disappeared.

"Nah, we talk about everything. That bitch forced him into that engagement. She wasn't important to him. That's why he didn't tell me about her," I thought as I began to smile.

I overreacted for nothing. Lamar and I were perfectly fine. I felt so stupid for destroying my room because I was going to have to clean this destruction up. Feeling more at ease, I logged out of all the social media that I had logged into. Killed all the apps and erased my history. I'd clean this mess up later. I caused my body unnecessary tension. It was now time for me to relax.

CHAPTER 5

I submerged myself in my jacuzzi styled tub with bubbles, lavender oil, chamomile oil and Epsom salt. The hot relaxing water sent me to a place where I hadn't been to in a long time, a place of peace. The pressure of the jets beat the kinks out of my body better than any deep tissue massage I ever had.

"I worked myself into a tizzy for nothing. Lamar and I are good. This was all I needed. Wish I had a blunt." I said to myself as I sipped my red wine.

After thirty minutes in the hot relaxing water, I could feel myself starting to slip away. To avoid slipping under the water and becoming a casualty, I turned the jets off, got out of the tub, and grabbed my fluffy towel. I was so relaxed that I had no idea how I was going to raise my feet to walk to my bed.

Doing a slow drag, I walked fifteen feet from my bathroom and stood in front of the floor length mirror beside my bed. Looking at myself with my pink fluffy towel in one hand and a glass of wine in the other hand, I was conflicted.

By my standards, I was beautiful. Flawless skin, large heavy breast with dark chocolate nipples. Flat stomach with a small waist that flared out into wide hips and a perfectly plump ass. Not that fake store-bought shit like Penelope. I thought I was perfect. But if that were true, why did I feel so flawed?

Though my body was near perfection. The men that were supposed to love me, chose woman that were nothing like me. I was a certified thick chick. The size 16 jeans that I wore hugged my body like a glove. But Kamiya, the woman my husband cheated on me with, was no bigger than a size 3.

This Andrea bitch was probably a size 5. Maybe a size 7, depending on the brand of the jeans.

"They're nothing like me," I whispered to myself as the water from the tub dripped down my body and the water from my eyes dripped down my face. I was slipping and my battle with depression was winning.

As I fought with myself. I could feel eyes on me, but I was too engrossed in my reflection to turn away. My door was closed, and I didn't recall hearing David coming in.

The scent of Burberry for men swept over my nose and caused goosebumps to appear on my skin. A clear sign that David had entered my room. The goosebumps that I used to get for him were from excitement. The goosebumps that were on my skin now, were from disgust.

All the tension that the jacuzzi jets had worked from my body was back. Opening the towel to cover myself, David came up beside me and removed it from my hand. He loomed over me as he came and stood behind me in the mirror. With his left hand, he rubbed the water that was on my stomach.

"He still wears his wedding band." I thought to myself as his smooth hands ran across my bare skin.

His dick was standing at attention in his black Jordan basketball shorts. Removing his hand from my wet skin, he stroked himself as if his hand could give him what

I used to give him. I hadn't touched David in over a year, and I didn't have plans on touching him tonight.

Something as natural as being nude in front of my husband felt wrong. I felt unclean, naked, and exposed. I felt like I was cheating on Lamar having another man see me this way. I attempted to move, but David grabbed my arm lightly, yet firm enough for me to feel. Firm enough to let me know that I wasn't going anywhere.

"You're drenched," he said as he bent his tall frame down and kissed my collar bone. I recoiled under his touch, if he noticed he didn't show it.

"Remember how I used to dry you off when we first got married? As soon as you stepped out of the shower, I'd be waiting with a fluffy towel." David said as he lightly dabbed my skin with the towel.

I didn't move from my spot in front of the mirror. Through the reflection, I could see his light eyes change to a darker color. Which let me know that he wasn't taking no for an answer tonight.

If the look in his eyes wasn't a clear enough sign, the fact that he dropped his boxer briefs and basketball shorts allowing his thick extremely hard manhood to rub against me was a dead giveaway. I had seen this look several times in our five years of marriage, back then I loved it. But now, not so much.

I was ashamed that he was seeing me with no clothes on. I felt vulnerable. I wanted to cover myself, but every time I reached for the towel, he gripped it tighter. He caused our disconnect, now he had to live with the consequences of his actions. I was Lamar's girl now and he needed to accept that and move on. I refused to say a word to him. We had nothing to talk about.

"It's been torturing Crystal. I haven't been inside of you in over a year," he said as he sat on the edge of my bed. Pulling me between his legs and sucking one of my very large breast into his mouth. He moaned deeply as he ran his hands all over my body.

He sucked on my nipples like he was a starving baby and dragged his thick wet tongue over my entire body. I could feel his body relax as if he were holding his breath. Little did he know, I was about to bring the stress right back to his ass.

He didn't deserve peace. Not after what he had done to me. I could tell he was enjoying himself. His jagged breathing, his masculine hands roaming and squeezing my body, and his dick jumping like he was about to cum on himself were all tell-tale signs.

I knew my husband, and the thought of another woman knowing his mannerisms hurt more than he'd ever know. Kamiya had one up'ed me. So, he could take his ass back to her. As soon as he placed his warm mouth and wet tongue on my pussy, I backed up and began to speak.

"I don't want this, David. I want a divorce. I don't want alimony or spousal support. I don't want your money. I don't want this house. I just want to be happy again. I want peace. I deserve it." I said as tears sprang to my eyes.

This was the first time that I had spoken to him without arguing and yelling. I spoke to him from the calmness in my heart. We were over and by the stillness that came over him he knew it too. He had done something that couldn't be fixed. Inhaling and exhaling as if he were trying to still his anger. He gripped my waist harder than he ever had before.

"Ahhhh!!!" I screamed as his strong fingers dug into my flesh.

"Crystal, why the fuck are you doing this? I know I fucked up in the worst way. I'm so sorry. I should've never asked you to get rid of our kids. Looking around this room, I can tell that seeing Nyla's stuff sent you over the edge. I messed up, but you gotta know I love you.

We're not the first couple to go through this. I've been trying to give you the space that you need to come back to me. But I'm not giving you space to divorce me. You can cancel that. You're my wife." David said as he glared at me. The lust that was in his eyes earlier were replaced by anger. The grip that he had on me was so hard that I knew I would be bruised.

"We're done Dav...Ahhh" before I could finish saying what I was about to say. David stood up quickly, wrapped his strong hand around my throat and damn near crushed my windpipe. I scratched and clawed at his hand, but he was unbothered. He was too angry to care that I had ripped the skin off his hand with my nails.

"Bitch I know what this is. Did you call yourself getting back at me? Did you cheat on me Crystal? Did you fuck some other nigga like a hoe?" David asked. The anger that was just in his eyes was gone.

This was a raged look. David had never put his hands on me, and he had never called me anything other than Crystal or Beautiful. The presence of the term bitch and his hand around my throat, let me know he would beat my ass.

I may have been angry, but I was not a fool. I didn't know for sure what was on the other side of this look, and I wasn't about to fuck around and find out. Admitting to fucking Lamar would never come out of my mouth.

"The only hoe in here is you. No other nigga has ever been inside of me." I croaked as I matched his menacing stare. After a minute his features softened, and he released me. I fell to the floor and grabbed my sore throat. I couldn't believe that this man had put his hands on me.

"It's obvious that I don't know you anymore. The man that I married would've never caused so much pain in my life. I still want a divorce." I cried as I sat on the floor with a broken heart and sore throat. I could feel David staring at me. He was conflicted.

"I'm sorry Beautiful." He said as he lightly grabbed a handful of my hair, lifted me off the floor and pushed me onto the bed. The lust that was originally in his eyes was now   back.

CHAPTER 6

"How did we get here?" I asked myself. As I felt my clit begin to swell. I refused to have sex with this man. He had multiple bitches vying for his attention. He didn't need me.

"I'm serious David. We're done." I said as I tried to force my tears to stop falling.

"Nah, we're not getting a divorce. You're my wife and I'll never allow another man to have you." He said as he climbed on the bed and latched onto my pussy. I nearly jumped off the bed at the initial contact of his mouth. Head had never felt so good. Lamar gave me head every time we had sex, but it didn't feel like this.

"Mmmm." David moaned as he devoured me. His soft lips and soft wet tongue felt so good I wanted to cry. I could feel the love, but I no longer wanted it. But I'd let him get this nut, because after this sex session was over, he'd never get another one. Raising both of my legs, I placed them behind my head.

Whoever said thick chicks weren't flexible had surely lied. I was folded up like a pretzel, and David loved it. Grabbing his head, I rode his mouth until I felt myself begin to squirt.

"Ohhh God!" I screamed as David continued to lick my overly sensitive twat. Watching him suck on my pussy with a face full of cum was the sexiest thing that I had ever seen.

"Please. Please stop." I begged as I tried to push his head away. I was too weak to move.

"Nah, you taste so good." He said as he stiffened his tongue and fucked me with it. I couldn't take it anymore. It took me beating him in his head for him to stop. He knew what he was doing to me.

"Are you ready for me? I need you, Crystal." He said as he slapped his thick heavy dick on my clit. I hated to admit it, but I was in ecstasy, and he knew it. I couldn't even speak; all I could do was nod my head yes. We held each other's gaze as he prepared to enter me for the first time in over a year. I watched his face twist up in ecstasy as I spread my pussy lips open for him to enter.

"Ahhhh!!" I screamed and he moaned as he guided his dick inside of me. I had forgotten just how big he was, and he had obviously forgotten how tight I was. He moved in and out of me slowly at first, then aggressively.

Tears ran down my face as my husband beat my G-spot like it stole something. I loved it and I didn't want him to stop. For the first time in over a year, I was confused. I was in love with Lamar. But listening to David moan and call my name was doing something to me. It felt so good rubbing my hands over my husband's hard body.

"I gotta pull out or I'ma cum too early. It's too tight. Damn Crystal." David said as he pulled out of me and tried to calm himself down. I was enjoying him, but I wasn't foolish enough to believe that sex would change anything.

I still hated him, but his dick covered with my cum had me foaming at the mouth. All I wanted to do was suck him dry, but I didn't.

"I missed you," I admitted as he laid me on my side and snuggled behind me. Spooning me, he slid his mammoth sized girth in my ass causing me to whimper. It hurt like hell at first, but the way he massaged my clit and kissed my neck made the pain less noticeable.

"I missed you too. We don't need a divorce. All we need is each other and our future kids. I'ma make everything right again. I swear." He said as he began to pump hard inside my backdoor. The moment he was about to cum, he pulled out of my ass and rammed his pulsating dick back inside my pussy.

"God damn." David screamed as he released his nut deep inside of me. Continuing to pump hard until his balls were empty. I could feel his heart beating out of control as the aftershock of an amazing sex session caused him to shake uncontrollably.

"David, I…"

"Shhh. Let's just go to sleep. I'll call the cleaning service in the morning to clean this room. I love you, Crystal. It's me, you, and whatever kid God decides to bless us with in the next nine months." David slurred. It was obvious that he had worn himself out. He pulled me close to him and immediately fell asleep. A full minute hadn't passed before I heard soft snoring behind me. His embrace felt right, but I knew better.

I was not going to let good sex change my mind. Our sex life was always good. I wasn't going to let him get away with what he had done to me. If I let it slip once, he'd continue to do the same thing all over again. I had moved on.

Looking at the clock on the nightstand, I saw that it was after midnight. I lay next to David for three hours before I got out of bed. He didn't move. He always slept like a log after we had sex and cuddled.

Getting out of bed and grabbing his iPhone out of his basketball shorts. I raised his right hand and placed his thumb on the sensor to unlock his cell phone. I already knew what I was going to find, but I still needed to see.

I went straight to his photos and found what I knew I would find. Naked pictures of him, naked pictures of random bitches, and videos of him having sex. I wasn't bothered because for the full year he and I had not been together. The pictures that stood out the most to me were the pictures he had of me. David had taken pictures of me as I slept and while I was going to work.

"Was he stalking me?" I asked myself. The pictures of me sleeping were in the guess room that I now occupied. He had been sneaking in my room, lying next to me, and taken pictures of us in bed. That had to be the creepiest thing I ever saw.

Exiting his pictures, I went through his text messages. I wasn't surprised at the tons of messages from more random bitches. Sex talk and dick pictures seemed to be all his phone was filled with. Looking through his and Kamiya's message I was shocked at the level of hate between the two of them.

To: David From: Kamiya *I swear to God. You ain't nothing but a bitch ass nigga. Your daughter needs shit and you're acting like a measly $1000 a week can take care of her needs.*

To: Kamiya From: David *Bitch fuck you. Sack chasing ass. Why the fuck does a one-year-old even need $4000.00 a month? My child support is not for your other kids. If you can't understand that, me and my wife can take Nyla.*

To: David From: Kamiya *Fuck you. I wish I never sat on your dick.*

To: Kamiya From: David *I wish you didn't either. Fucking coke head.*

I smiled at all the hell she was putting him through. He deserved it. Closing his text messages. I went over to his Facebook Messenger. My heart cracked in half when I saw two people that I knew in his inbox.

"How could he?" I asked myself as I read through messages from both Penelope and Trinity. Even though I suspected that he would be the type of person to fuck bitches that I work with, I didn't really want it to be true. I wanted to believe that he cared for me a little, but I knew now that he didn't. Shaking my head, I opened the messages and began to read.

FB Message from Penelope Scranton: *Look, I'm tired of being your side bitch. After two years I feel like I deserve more. You said you were leaving Crystal. But I always catch you sneaking through the job parking lot, and I always hear you calling her office line. Explain or I will tell her about us.*

FB Message from David Jones: *Bitch don't threaten me. I never told you I was leaving my wife. I'll never leave her. Try and get cute and I'll send you back to the Section 8 projects where I found you. Don't bite the hand that feeds you.*

Tears rushed to my eyes. David had no respect for me. The fact that he would sleep with the women I worked with, let me know just how he felt about me. He didn't care how uncomfortable a situation like that would be for me. I was obviously a sucker for pain because soon after I read the messages between him and Penelope, I went to Trinity's messages.

FB Message from David Jones: I haven't touched my wife in almost a year. Is she fucking somebody in y'all office.

FB Message from Trinity Harlow: No. She's not and what does it matter if she is or isn't? I thought you wanted to be with me. I've been following her just like you asked, but she never does anything. If you don't trust her, leave her alone. She'll be just fine without you. I left my fiancé for you. Now, I'm all alone and struggling. Please, David. I need you.

FB Message from David Jones: I'm not leaving my wife. We already discussed this. I trust Crystal. Just making sure she's not as scandalous as the people she works with.

FB Message from Trinity Harlow: I hope Crystal opens her eyes one day and sees that you ain't shit. I know several niggas in the office that want to fuck her. She'd be better off if she was as scandalous as the people she worked with. Fuck you, David.

FB Message from David Jones: Who's trying to fuck my wife?

I had seen enough. The humiliation that I had endured at the hands of my own husband was too much. I cheated on Lamar tonight for no reason. The messages from Penelope and Trinity were dated two days ago. Looking at him sleeping peacefully pissed me off.

Before I knew what I was doing, I threw the phone hard and cracked him in the face.

"WHAT THE FUCK?! What the fuck is wrong with you Crystal?!" David screamed as he jumped from the bed. Still naked and glistening from our sex session a few hours earlier.

"You son of a bitch! You've been fucking my coworkers? You came in here and fucked me knowing you were fucking bitches that sit in my face every day!!" I screamed as I threw punches all over his well chiseled body. The look on his face was genuine shock as he looked at his opened phone. There was no lie that he could tell to fix this.

"Baby, stop. Crystal I'm…"

"Fuck you, David. I fucking hate you." I screamed as I grabbed my purse. I had a man that really did care about me. I didn't have to take this level of disrespect from my soon to be ex-husband.

"Crystal, I'm sorry baby. I don't care about any of those bitches. Things just got out of hand. You know how scandalous hoes get down. I was trying to keep tabs on you and one thing led to another. I don't want them bitches Crystal." He said as he grabbed my hand. Panic registered in his voice and all over his face, but I didn't care. I was done. I could do bad by myself. I didn't need him for that.

"Just an FYI. I have been fucking someone…"

SLAP!!!

Before I could even finish my sentence, David slapped me so hard that I flew into my floor length mirror. The look of rage, betrayal, and pain contorted his face into something that made pee seep from my bladder.

"Bitch, I'll kill you." He said as he dropped to his knees and used both of his hands to choke me.

"I'll kill you before I let another man have…AHHHH!!!" David screamed in pain when I grabbed the biggest piece of the broken lamp and stabbed him repeatedly until I felt his grip loosen around my neck. My lungs burned as I gasped for air.

"David. I…" Panic gripped me as I saw what I had done to him. Blood was everywhere.

"Call 9-1-1 Crystal. Tell them someone broke into the house and attacked me when they couldn't find the safe. I know you didn't mean to do this. It'll be ok Beautiful." David said in a raspy voice. The painful look on his face nearly crippled me.

"He's trying to help me stage this. He does love me." I thought to myself, as I applied pressure to the wound in his stomach.

"This is my chance to be free. If he lives, he'll never give me the divorce I want. This is my chance to rid myself of David Jones. It's the only way for Lamar and I to be together. I can't call 9-1-1." I thought to myself as I stared into his pained green eyes.

"I'm sorry David." I said as I leaned over and kissed him. Thick globs of blood came out of his mouth as he coughed. He was obviously in pain.

"It's ok Crystal. You won't go down for this. I promise. Call the police and tell them what I told you to say. We can get through this. I love you," he said as he stared into my eyes. Tears clouded my vision at his words.

"I love you too Baby. *'Til death do us part*," I said as I picked up the broken lamp and began to stab him until life was no longer present in his beautiful green eyes.

I cried but this was his fault. If he had loved me the right way, I would've never fallen in love with another man and have to erase him from my life.

CHAPTER 7

Looking at the clock, I saw that it was 7am. I was up all-night bathing David. He was never the type to be seen poorly dressed or unkempt. So, after bathing him. I patched his wounds with gauze and thick white towels. Then went over them with saran wrap. I didn't want any blood to soil his fresh white Tee.

After bathing and dressing him. I brushed his soft wavy hair and kissed his cold lips. Even in death, he was still the most handsome man that I had ever seen, next to Lamar.

"I'm sorry things had to be this way, David. All I wanted was to be with the man I loved. But you were being so selfish. All you had to do was sign the damn papers. I told you; I didn't want your money. All I wanted was my happiness.

I'm going to be in the other room. I have so much to do today. So, I need to get started. I have some calls to make. But I'll be right back. If you need anything, just call my name." I said to my deceased husband as I kissed him again and walked into his bedroom.

I hadn't been in the room that he and I once shared in over a year. The bed was unmade as usual. As I looked around, old memories began to play in my head. David and I had made love in every inch of this room. From the bed to the wall, the floor, and the closet. Everything looked the same, yet so different. The multiple pictures of me on the nightstand on his side of the bed was a new addition. Pictures that I never took.

"Are those surveillance pictures?" I asked myself. I looked at pictures that appeared to be taken from a distance. Pictures of me in the mall, at the park reading, or walking into the hair salon. I shook my head at the thought that this man was really following me. I can remember several times in the past when he called me, asking where I was.

"What's up Beautiful?" David said into the receiver.

"Hey." I said unenthusiastically. If he caught the disinterest in my tone, he didn't show it. He continued to talk like I wasn't brushing him off or ignoring him.

"I was in my office thinking about the times you and I would go to the park. And how I used to eat you on the bench behind the bushes, then slid inside your wet pussy like people weren't outside," he said. The lust in his voice was evident.

I couldn't lie and say I wasn't turned on especially since at the time of his call the park was where I was. David had a mouth from God, but I no longer wanted it.

"David, listen…"

"Why are you depriving me, Crystal? It's killing me not being able to make you cum. I'm on my way over there just so I can feel your presence." David said and hung up.

I chuckled at the memory. Because he knew where I was the whole time.

"If you were a better husband, you'd still be alive." I said.

Grabbing the cordless phone off the base beside my old king-sized bed. I called St. Mary's Hospital.

"St. Mary's Memorial Human Resource Department. This is Gladys." A kind voice said into the phone.

"Good morning, Gladys. This is Brenda from Floral Delights. I have two dozen red and pink roses along with an Edible Arrangement to be delivered to Ms. Andrea Turner. Is she available to accept the delivery?" I said into the phone. After taking care of David, I logged back into my Facebook account and went to Andrea's page.

Going to the About section, I saw that Andrea was the Human Resource Director for the hospital. It was about time I let her know to stay away from my man.

"I swear Lamar has to be the sweetest young man of all time. He always has flowers and goodies sent here for Andrea. I told her if I were thirty years younger, I'd have to give her a run for her money." Gladys said and laughed.

Rage filled me like never before. Lamar had never sent me a damn thing. Yeah, he may have bought me lunch a few times, but flowers and goodies were not amongst the things that I got from him.

"From the looks of these bouquets she's a very lucky woman." I said as I tried to keep the anger out of my voice.

"Well Brenda, Andrea won't be here until 11. But I'll leave a..."

Before Gladys could finish her sentence, I hung up on her. I didn't need to hear that she would leave her a message. I had already gotten all the info that I needed. Since she wasn't at work, I'd go to their home.

I had trailed Lamar home enough to know where he lived. On several occasions, I even rode through his parking lot to see if he was home alone. Since I didn't know he was fucking around back then, I didn't think that the other cars parked near his car belonged to a person that resided in his home.

"I was good to this motherfucker, and he thought he could play me." I said to myself as I got ready to take a shower. I sent him several messages after I left work yesterday and he hadn't replied to any of my messages. Normally when I messaged him, he responded within fifteen minutes. Now that I was asking questions about things he should've told me about earlier, he was dodging me like a bill collector.

Every day for the past three years Lamar and I had deep conversations. We talked about everything from me feeling unattractive, my failed marriage, my abortions, and my fear of never being a mother.

In addition to my baggage, we discussed his parents, his kids, and how he wanted to open different businesses in the city. He didn't want to continue making another person's company grow when he could be focusing on his own dreams.

Because I believed in his dreams, I put him in contact with a realtor I knew from college. He found several profitable locations for his future barber shop, beauty salon, and restaurant. We discussed important life situations, problems, and events. So, the fact that he never mentioned Andrea Turner, let me know that she really wasn't important.

For my own sanity, I needed to know why I had to find out that she even existed from my husband's mouthy side bitch. We had shared too much, done too much, and confided in each other too much for us to have any secrets.

On several occasions Lamar told me how much he was in love with my pussy, and how much he needed me because I made him feel whole. What we had extended past our work schedule. He knew it just as well as I did. We were soulmates. The sooner he realized that and stopped making that skinny bitch think otherwise, the better off he and I would be.

Hopping into the shower that David had his contractors custom build for me, I stood under the powerful shower head and let the downpour of water beat the tension out of my body.

I massaged my large breast and hard nipples as I thought about the last time Lamar, and I made love. Lamar commanded respect when he was laying his pipe game down. With the waterproof vibrating shower sponge that I purchased from www.AdamandEve.com, I held the sponge against my sensitive pussy.

Thoughts of Lamar and my sexcapades consumed my thoughts. Sex in his car, work bathroom, work stairwell and even the times he came to my home had me ready to erupt.

The pulsating shower, powerful vibrating sponge, and visions of my work husband sent me over the edge. The orgasm that swept over my body as I masturbated made my knees buckle, causing me to fall to the shower floor.

"Oh my God!!!" I panted as I twitched on the tile floor of the shower. My skin was so sensitive that the water began to feel like needle pricks on my skin. Dragging myself up and standing on wobbly legs, I used the wall to steady myself and turned the water off.

By the time I got out of the shower, covered my entire body with baby oil, lotion, and sprayed on my perfume. I was ready to confront my man about the secrets he had been keeping.

Walking back into my room, I saw that a small red stain was now present on David's fresh white Tee. But I didn't have time to change it. Looking at the clock, I saw that it was 7:57am. I had to go.

"I know you don't like being unclean. But I'm busy right now. I'll change your clothes when I get back." I said to David. Then grabbed my purse and walked out the door.

CHAPTER 8

As soon as I got in my car, I activated Bluetooth and called Lamar. I wanted to know why he hadn't responded to any of my messages. The iPhone indicator let me know exactly what time he read my messages. So did Snapchat and Messenger. Even the Instagram DMs said 'seen' when he opened my messages. So why was he now giving me his ass to kiss?

We were so much better than this, and if he thought that he could ignore me and I would just take it, he was sadly mistaken. I had given him too much of me for him to brush me off like I was nothing more than a cheap thrill.

"Siri. Call Monica."

"Calling Monica."

Listening to the phone ring, I could feel my pulse rate quicken. All I wanted to do was hear his voice. Then…

'Leave the kid a message. BEEP'

"No, this nigga didn't." I screamed as I pounded the steering wheel of my car. Hearing the phone ring once then go straight to voicemail. Pissed me off.

I knew like everybody knew that this nigga kept his phone no more than two inches away from his hand. Meaning it was always in reach. So, the fact that he had just ignored my call. Wasn't sitting well with me.

I drove my 2019 Lexus LC 500 to Lamar's townhouse subdivision like a bat out of hell. I made the usual 40-minute drive in less than 25 minutes. He had a lot of explaining to do.

Pulling up to Peaceful Waters Townhouse community, all I saw were children riding their bikes, people walking their dogs, and overall friendly smiling faces. This community looked like a place of peace and serenity, but not for long.

Finding the nearest parking space, I went back to Andrea's page and strolled through all her visible pictures to see if I could find a picture of her car.

"Bingo." I said as I found a picture from February 14. The description said, *'He doesn't have to say I love you, when he shows me every day. #IGOTTHEKEYS #2018NISSANALTIMA #HELOVESME.*

"You bought that bitch a car? A fucking car!!" I screamed as I looked at the gunmetal colored car. I was so mad that I threw my phone against my passenger side window. Causing it to crack in a spider web pattern.

My heart raced as I looked at the car. All Lamar gave me for Valentine's Day was a sore back from having his dick and balls deep inside my ass and a simple 'Happy Valentine's Day Baby' text. What really pissed me off was the fact that I had seen this car in the parking lot every time I drove through this nigga's complex.

Looking around the parking lot, I spotted Lamar's Silver Lincoln Continental and parked directly beside it was the 2018 Nissan Altima that was in the picture.

"Did you really think I was going to let some bitch come in on what we have? You belong to me Lamar. It's show time nigga." I said to myself as I looked in the mirror to make sure my makeup was flawless. This Andrea character needed to know that she didn't hold a candle to me.

I was the person that Lamar confided in. I was the woman that he shared his dreams with. I was the main lady and she had to go. I got out of my car wearing a black halter dress and black and white Chuck Taylor's. Lamar loved it when I wore this dress. Checking my reflection one last time, I walked up to his townhouse. He had a choice to make. And if he knew like I knew, he'd better choose wisely.

I stood outside the burgundy door of his townhouse, listening to the sound of laughter and children playing. I could clearly hear Lamar laughing too. Pulling my phone out, I called his phone once again.

"Daddy your phone is ringing!" I heard one of his daughters say.

"Who is it?" Lamar asked.

"It says bill collector." The child said.

"Hit the red button Rissa." He shouted.

"No, the fuck he didn't just say that." I said to myself. I was furious. This nigga had my number saved as fucking bill collector. Since he wanted to try and act like I wasn't important, I was about to make my presence known.

It was after 8am. I had no idea why his kids weren't on their way to school. But, since he wanted to keep them home, they'd have to learn that their daddy wasn't shit.

Knocking on the door, I turned the knob then walked in. I could smell the pungent aroma of his weed and the sweet smell of pancakes and syrup as soon as I opened the front door. Now I knew this was a peaceful neighborhood because black people never left their doors unlocked.

"Babe, was somebody at the door? Or was that Mari and Rissa beating on something." I heard a woman say. I assumed it was that bitch, Andrea. I didn't like how comfortable and relaxed this bitch sounded talking to my man.

"Nah, that was Rissa and them beating on that Karaoke thing." Lamar said.

"Lamar, you sound crazy. Why the fuck would they be beating on the karaoke machine?" Andrea asked.

"I don't fucking know DD. Why the fuck do they do any of the shit they do in here? Because they're bad, damn. Now come sit on this dick while they're upstairs." He ordered.

The sound of her giggling, then moaning, made my body temperature rise. If he thought he was going to fuck this bitch, he was sadly mistaken.

"WOWWW!!! SO, THIS IS HOW YOU DO ME LAMAR!" I screamed as I ran into the den where my man's big bear sized ass was fucking that anorexic bitch. The sight of that bony bitch sitting on top of my man with her small B cup breast in his mouth pissed me off. The two of them didn't even look good together. I ran to the couch attempting to tackle her off his dick.

"WHAT THE FUCK?!" Lamar screamed as he jumped off the couch. His dick was rock hard and wet from where he had pulled out of her. He protectively pushed her behind him, then stuffed his now soft dick back in his sweatpants.

"Are you kidding me. You're fucking this bony bitch raw. Who is this bitch, Lamar?" I screamed, trying to get around him to attack her. Females needed to learn that they couldn't go around fucking other people's property.

"Crystal? Yo, what the fuck are you doing in my house?" Lamar screamed.

"Oh, you know me now? I'm not 'Bill Collector' now? I've been calling you and messaging you all fucking night. Who the fuck is this bitch?" I asked again.

"Crystal? You're coworker? Why the fuck is she in my house?" Andrea asked. The fury on her face as she looked between me, and Lamar was comical to me.

"That's right bitch. It's obvious that you know who I am. Who the fuck are you? Who is this bitch, Lamar?" I asked, there was no need to even address her at this point. Because it was obvious, she knew the role I played in his life.

"Bitch, I don't know how the fuck you know where I live. But you better get your ass out of my house." Lamar screamed.

I was shocked by the way he was glaring at me. I looked behind me to see if someone else was behind me because I knew he could not have been glaring at me the way he was.

"Lamar, so you gonna try to show out for this bony bitch. Nigga you just fucked me yesterday now you're trying to stunt. Sweetheart, I been knowing Lamar for years and I never heard of you. You were obviously just something to do when he wasn't doing me. Tell her the truth Lamar. Tell her how you fuck the lining out my pussy and eat my ass. Tell her that you love me." I said, matching his glare.

"What is she talking about Lamar?" De' Andrea asked as tears came to her eyes.

"DD don't listen to her. She's lying. I don't give a fuck about her. She was just somebody to talk to at work I never touched this bitch. Go upstairs with the girls and call the police. Tell them some crazy bitch broke in the house."

Call the police. Tell them some crazy bitch broke in the house.

Call the police. Tell them somebody broke in the house.

His words echoed in my head. Reverberating off each corner of my mind. Images of a bleeding David staring at me with his green eyes, saying those same words to me before I killed him to be with Lamar. David was trying to protect me. Lamar was trying to convict me. Confusion caused my head to ache.

"No. You love me, Lamar. You told me you love me." I screamed as I paced back and forth in his large den.

"Bitch, I don't…"

"Daddy, can you reach the cookies?" A little girl said as she ran into the den.

"Mari go upstairs." Lamar said with panic lacing his voice.

The fear that seeped out in his voice and covered his face was unlike anything I had ever seen before. I knew without the shadow of a doubt that he loved this little girl more than me or the bitch behind him. That was all I needed to know to get my point across.

As soon as the little girl rounded the corner, I grabbed her by her tiny wrist and snatched her close to me.

"Oh God!! Please let my baby go." Andrea screamed as boulder size teardrops came to her eyes. I didn't give a fuck about her tears. If she and these Rugrats weren't in the picture. Lamar wouldn't be playing hard to get. I ignored her tears; this was between me and Lamar.

"Do you know what I had to do for us to be together? You just told Trinity you had love for me. I love you. Now you're talking to me like I ain't shit. Like I didn't mean anything to you." I screamed as tears ran down my face. Images of David staring up at me with his blank green eyes played on repeat in my head.

"Crystal. Listen. I like you. But I never said I loved you. Please let my baby girl go. She's just a kid. She didn't do anything." Lamar begged as his eyes began to glisten.

"*Like me?*" I scoffed. "You said you loved me. I killed my husband for you. I killed David for us." I screamed as snot and tears ran down my face. The look of terror on his face and the wailing from Andrea made me laugh hysterically. Lamar played me, but I'd get the last laugh.

"Crystal. I never…"

"How about now? Do you love me now?" I asked as I pulled the small handgun out of my thigh holster and pointed it at Lamaria's head. The little girl wailed and hollered as she struggled to get away from me, but I refused to let her go.

"Oh God." Andrea and Lamar screamed. But I didn't care. They needed to feel the pain that Lamar had caused me. The fear on his face made my pussy wet.

"Yes, I love you. I love you, Crystal. We can be together. I don't want Andrea. We can leave here right now. Just don't hurt my daughter." Lamar said as he dropped to his knees begging.

That was all I wanted to hear him say, but his actions showed me he didn't mean it. He was just playing with me again. Fool me once shame on you. Fool me twice shame on me. I was done playing the fool.

"You played with my heart Lamar. You won't be alone Lamaria. My babies are in Heaven too." I said as I pulled the trigger and ended Lamaria's young life.

"Noooo!!" Lamar and Andrea screamed as they cradled their daughter's dead body. Her tiny frame lay crumbled on the floor as blood covered their hardwood floor. Unlike him, I had a heart. I refused to let him suffer and feel misery. I loved him too much for that.

"I did this because I love you." I said as I placed the handgun to the back of his head and pulled the trigger again and again. Leaving him, his daughter, and that knock off bitch in a heap on the floor.

"If I couldn't have you. No one could have you." I said and smiled. Then took a seat on the couch and called 9-1-1.

EPILOGUE

"If Lamar knew he didn't want to be with me, he shouldn't have made me fall in love with him. He played me. That's why I did it." I said to the 911 operator after I gave her full details of the last 24 hours of my life.

I looked at the mini massacre that I had created in Lamar's home and felt no remorse. He knew that I needed love, and he knew that I was in love with him. If he wasn't willing to give me the love I needed, then he shouldn't have crossed the line from my coworker to my lover.

I could hear his daughter Larissa stifle her crying. She must've thought I was coming for her. But I wasn't. The states could handle her once they threw her ass in foster care.

"Ma'am is this a prank call. 9-1-1 is for emergency's only." The operator said.

"No, it's not a prank call." I said calmly. "I really killed my husband David Jones so that I could be with my work husband. My husband David is at our home at 5726 Spindle Lane. You'll find him upstairs in the 3rd bedroom from the bathroom."

"Ma'am are you sure your husband is deceased."

"Quite sure. Like I said. I killed Lamar too. But I spared the life of one of his children. She's still alive somewhere in this house. I'm just not in the mood to look for her." I said lighting the blunt that Lamar had in the ash tray.

"Ma'am, are you saying there are survivors at 115 Peaceful Lane?"

"Yes, just one more other than me. But by the time you get here. She'll be the only survivor. I don't want to live without Lamar." I said as I exhaled the weed smoke.

"Ma'am, emergency responders are on the way to both locations. Please stay on..."

"Let me leave you with some parting words before I go." I said cutting the operator off. "Never sleep with any of the men that you work with. Everything they tell you, will be a lie." I said and ended the call.

Inhaling the last bit of weed smoke. I braced myself for the end. Everyone I loved was in heaven. My two babies, David, now Lamar. Lamar thought death could separate us. He was sadly mistaken. Not even death could keep me away from him.

"I'm on my way." I said as I drew a cross over my heart, put the gun to my head. Then pulled the trigger.

The End

Thank you for reading **Work Husband.** This book was written by Octavia Grant. If you're interested in finding out about upcoming projects and new releases, please connect with the author via social media:

Facebook: Octavia Taneka Grant
Facebook: Author Octavia Grant
Instagram: @Otaneka
TikTok: @Otaneka

octaviatgrant@gmail.com

Be sure to check out the author's other short stories, standalones, and series by searching **Octavia Grant** on Amazon or by clicking the link https://www.amazon.com/-/e/B06WW7WRDK to access the author's Amazon Page, and please leave a review.

Printed in Great Britain
by Amazon

40907762R00037